The Boxcar Children Mysteries

THE BOXCAR CHILDREN
SURPRISE ISLAND
THE YELLOW HOUSE MYSTERY
MYSTERY RANCH
MIKE'S MYSTERY
BLUE BAY MYSTERY
THE WOODSHED MYSTERY
THE LIGHTHOUSE MYSTERY
MOUNTAIN TOP MYSTERY
SCHOOLHOUSE MYSTERY
CABOOSE MYSTERY
HOUSEBOAT MYSTERY
SNOWBOUND MYSTERY
TREE HOUSE MYSTERY
BICYCLE MYSTERY
MYSTERY IN THE SAND
MYSTERY BEHIND THE WALL
BUS STATION MYSTERY
BENNY UNCOVERS A MYSTERY
THE HAUNTED CABIN
   MYSTERY
THE DESERTED LIBRARY
   MYSTERY
THE ANIMAL SHELTER
   MYSTERY
THE OLD MOTEL MYSTERY
THE MYSTERY OF THE HIDDEN
   PAINTING
THE AMUSEMENT PARK
   MYSTERY
THE MYSTERY OF THE MIXED-
   UP ZOO

THE CAMP-OUT MYSTERY
THE MYSTERY GIRL
THE MYSTERY CRUISE
THE DISAPPEARING FRIEND
   MYSTERY
THE MYSTERY OF THE SINGING
   GHOST
MYSTERY IN THE SNOW
THE PIZZA MYSTERY
THE MYSTERY HORSE
THE MYSTERY AT THE DOG
   SHOW
THE CASTLE MYSTERY
THE MYSTERY OF THE LOST
   VILLAGE
THE MYSTERY ON THE ICE
THE MYSTERY OF THE
   PURPLE POOL
THE GHOST SHIP MYSTERY
THE MYSTERY IN
   WASHINGTON, DC
THE CANOE TRIP MYSTERY
THE MYSTERY OF THE HIDDEN
   BEACH
THE MYSTERY OF THE MISSING
   CAT
THE MYSTERY AT SNOWFLAKE
   INN
THE MYSTERY ON STAGE
THE DINOSAUR MYSTERY
THE MYSTERY OF THE STOLEN
   MUSIC

The Mystery at the Ball Park
The Chocolate Sundae Mystery
The Mystery of the Hot Air Balloon
The Mystery Bookstore
The Pilgrim Village Mystery
The Mystery of the Stolen Boxcar
Mystery in the Cave
The Mystery on the Train
The Mystery at the Fair
The Mystery of the Lost Mine
The Guide Dog Mystery
The Hurricane Mystery
The Pet Shop Mystery
The Mystery of the Secret Message
The Firehouse Mystery

The Mystery in San Francisco
The Niagara Falls Mystery
The Mystery at the Alamo
The Outer Space Mystery
The Soccer Mystery
The Mystery in the Old Attic
The Growling Bear Mystery
The Mystery of the Lake Monster
The Mystery at Peacock Hall
The Windy City Mystery
The Black Pearl Mystery
The Cereal Box Mystery
The Panther Mystery
The Mystery of the Queen's Jewels
The Mystery of the Stolen Sword

THE MYSTERY OF THE STOLEN SWORD

created by
GERTRUDE CHANDLER WARNER

Illustrated by Charles Tang

ALBERT WHITMAN & Company
Morton Grove, Illinois

ISBN 0-8075-7623-9

9 10 8

Printed in the U.S.A.

Contents

CHAPTER   PAGE

1. A Ghost Story   1
2. The Orchard   12
3. The Missing Letters   21
4. The Secret Passageway   36
5. Veronica   43
6. Signs in the Orchard   55
7. A Stranger in the Library   68
8. The Antique Store   83
9. By the Light of the Moon   94
10. Joshua's Ghost   103

CHAPTER 1

A Ghost Story

Six-year-old Benny Alden stood outside his house in Greenfield, watching the moon rise. An owl hooted. Oak and maple trees rustled in the wind, and a few raindrops sprinkled Benny on the nose.

Benny shivered. In the moonlight, his front yard looked so spooky, he was almost sure he could see a ghost. And Benny definitely believed in ghosts.

It was early November, just a few days after Halloween. The leaves on the trees were yellow and brown, and many of the branches were almost bare. In the mornings, frost lay on the ground. The perfect season for ghosts, Benny thought.

"Benny, dinner's ready!" called a familiar voice. It was Benny's ten-year-old sister, Violet.

"Coming!" Benny called back. He took one more look at the moon before he raced inside.

"I'm starving," Benny announced to his family, who were already beginning to seat themselves at the long dining room table.

"You're always hungry, Benny," Henry reminded him with a smile. Henry was Benny's fourteen-year-old brother, and he could never resist teasing Benny a little.

Tonight Mrs. McGregor, the Aldens' housekeeper, had made one of Benny's favorite meals: spaghetti and meatballs, and her special homemade brownies for dessert.

Benny quickly slid into his seat next to his sister Jessie.

"How many meatballs, Benny?" asked Jessie as she put spaghetti on Benny's plate.

"Oh, maybe four," Benny answered.

"We can always count on you to have a good appetite, Benny," Grandfather remarked.

"I'll say," Henry agreed.

Jessie laughed but gave Benny all the meatballs he wanted. At age twelve, Jessie was the oldest girl in her family, and she often acted like a mother to her orphaned brothers and sister.

After their parents died Henry, Jessie, Violet, and Benny had lived in an abandoned boxcar in the woods because they thought they had nowhere else to go. They did not know that their grandfather was looking everywhere for them. When he finally found his missing grandchildren, he was overjoyed. And he lost no time inviting them to live with him — an offer the Aldens were happy to accept. Henry, Jessie, Violet, and Benny were especially pleased that Grandfather let them bring the old boxcar to his house, too. It was now in Grandfather's backyard, and the children often used it as a playhouse on rainy days.

Outside, the wind shook the trees, and a branch banged against the house.

Violet shuddered. "It's awfully windy tonight. Is there a storm coming?"

As if in answer, the lights in the house flickered but did not go out.

"The papers did say there would be a storm," Grandfather told his family as he stirred his tea.

"The kind with lots of thunder and lightning?" Benny asked hopefully.

"Nothing that dramatic, I'm afraid," Grandfather said.

"That's good." Violet sounded relieved. She looked around the dining room. The chandelier cast a soft glow on the walls and over the red-and-white-checked tablecloth. The smell of homemade tomato sauce mingled with that of the brownies baking in the oven.

As Mrs. McGregor cleared away the dinner plates, Grandfather leaned back in his chair. "I have some news," he told his grandchildren.

"What?" asked Benny, holding his cup in midair.

"Well . . ." Grandfather began slowly. "My friend Seymour Curtis called today. He'd like us to come visit him on his farm sometime this month."

"Is he the one who's always sending us fruit from his orchard?" asked Henry.

"He's the one," Grandfather answered, nodding.

"In fact," Mrs. McGregor added, "we just received a crate of apples from him this afternoon. I'll probably make apple pies with some of them tomorrow."

"Mmm," said Violet and Benny, almost in unison.

"Are there animals on this farm?" Benny wanted to know. "Or do they just grow fruit up there?"

"Oh, there are animals, Benny," his grandfather assured him. "The main business is the orchard, of course, but Seymour also keeps a few horses, cows, and a goat."

Benny beamed.

"And you know what else is on the farm?" Grandfather asked, looking at Benny.

"What?" Henry asked, just as eager to know.

"Well," Grandfather continued, "the orchard is supposedly haunted. At least that's what the townspeople think!"

Benny's eyes widened. "You mean there's a ghost?"

"Sort of," Grandfather said. "Everyone thinks the ghost of one of Seymour's ancestors haunts the farm — an ancestor who mysteriously vanished in the apple orchard one day and was never seen again."

"Oh, that's creepy!" Jessie exclaimed. "How long ago did this happen?"

"Oh, in the 1850s," answered Grandfather as the lights flickered overhead and the wind whipped the rain against the windowpanes. "In fact, he disappeared on a windy, rainy day like this. It was on the day after Halloween, I believe."

"And no one knows what happened to him?" Jessie couldn't believe it.

Grandfather shook his head. "No, no one ever found out."

"Who was this ancestor?" Henry wanted

to know. "And why did he just disappear like that? Was he running away from something? Or was it some kind of Halloween joke?"

"It wasn't much of a joke if no one ever saw him again," Violet remarked.

Grandfather leaned back in his chair. "Well, it's a long story," he began. "It all started in the middle of the last century when the farmhouse was first built."

Benny sat up straighter. He did not want to miss a word.

"The man who built the farm was an ancestor named Gideon Curtis, and he was rather eccentric."

"Ec-what?" asked Benny.

"Eccentric," Grandfather repeated. "He did some unusual things. For instance, he collected suits of armor and old swords, which he kept in a secret passageway he built in his farmhouse."

"Wow," said Benny. He was so interested in his grandfather's story, he was not even eating the brownie in front of him.

"This collection was very valuable,"

Grandfather continued. "So valuable that other people in Gideon's family wanted a share of it. One day, a relative from Virginia, a man named Joshua Curtis, came to visit Gideon. Joshua insisted that Gideon give him some swords from his collection, swords Joshua said belonged to his side of the family."

"Did they?" Jessie wondered aloud.

Grandfather shook his head. "Gideon didn't think so. He told Joshua he had no rightful claim to the swords. Joshua became very angry. He threatened Gideon and his family. Then he stormed out of the house, without any of his things, not even his coat. He walked into the orchard, and no one ever saw him again. It was as if he vanished."

"But people went out looking for him, didn't they?" Henry asked. He had barely touched his brownie, either.

"Oh, yes," Grandfather said as he poured cream into his tea. "Gideon and several men formed a search party. They looked for hours and hours. But no one ever found a trace of the man."

"Didn't he leave footprints?" Benny wanted to know.

"I'm sure he did," said Grandfather. "But none that ever led to his whereabouts. The townspeople believe that Joshua's ghost still haunts the orchard. And whenever Seymour has a poor harvest or other trouble on the farm, people blame the ghost. They say it's Joshua's revenge."

Benny's eyes grew very round. "You know, ghosts don't leave footprints," he informed his family. "Maybe that's why no one could find any sign of Joshua in the orchard."

"At that point he wasn't a ghost yet, Benny!" Jessie said, laughing.

"Did the ghost — I mean did Joshua — have a family in Virginia?" Violet asked.

"No, he never married and never had any children," Grandfather answered.

"How was Joshua related to Gideon?" Henry wondered as he poured more tea into his mug.

"They were cousins."

"How strange that Joshua just disappeared like that," Violet said. "I wonder what could have happened to him."

"It is an odd story," Grandfather agreed.

"Has anyone seen this ghost?" Henry wanted to know. "I mean, what makes people think the farm is haunted?"

Grandfather swallowed before he answered. "Some of the farmhands have heard strange noises in the orchard — leaves rustling even when there's no wind, the sound of twigs breaking in the underbrush, noises like that. Of course, it could just be some animal that people are hearing," Grandfather said.

Everyone nodded, except Benny. "I bet it's really a ghost," he insisted.

"We'll see," Grandfather said, chuckling.

"So when are we visiting?" Jessie wanted to know.

"We'll leave the day after tomorrow," Grandfather answered.

"Mmm," said Benny, taking a bite of his brownie.

CHAPTER 2

The Orchard

"Grandfather, we have to turn right at the next road," Jessie said. She sat in the front of the station wagon with a map unfolded in her lap.

The Aldens had been driving for almost three hours. It was now noon — "time for lunch," Benny reminded everyone. Watch, who was lying in the very back, thumped his tail.

"See, Watch is hungry, too," Benny announced.

"We'll be at the orchard by lunchtime,"

Grandfather said as he turned onto a narrow winding road. Acres and acres of fruit trees seemed to stretch for miles, broken only by fields where horses and cows grazed.

"Wow, there are a lot of orchards around here," Jessie commented. "All apples?"

"All apples," Grandfather answered.

"There's nothing on the trees now." Benny sounded disappointed as he looked at all the bare fruit trees.

"All the apples have been picked by this time," Grandfather explained. "Now Seymour is probably busy pruning the trees and cleaning up things around the barn."

"Does he need our help?" Benny asked.

"I'm sure Seymour would appreciate any help," Grandfather answered. "But this isn't a working vacation."

"Except that we have to look for the ghost," Benny reminded his family.

"And we can help feed the animals," Jessie suggested.

"Yes, you can probably do that," said Grandfather as he turned onto a dirt road.

"You can see the Curtis farm up ahead," he informed his grandchildren as he pointed to a big red barn in the distance. Around the barn was a big house and a long, low shed.

"It looks like all the buildings on the farm are connected," Henry observed. Grandfather was driving slowly now because there were deep ruts in the narrow dirt road.

"They are," Grandfather answered as he steered the car around a jagged rock in the road. "Farms that were built more than a hundred years ago often had connected buildings. They made for easy passage in the wintertime during those blinding snowstorms."

"Where is the secret passageway?" Benny wanted to know.

"Ah, that I'll let you find for yourself," Grandfather answered, "but I'll give you a hint. The secret passageway is underground."

"Underground," Benny repeated. He looked as if he didn't really believe it.

"Oh, look, a pumpkin patch," exclaimed

Violet, pointing, "and there're still pump-kins in it."

"They're huge," Jessie commented.

The Aldens were now passing a pasture where two horses pranced very close to the barn.

"And we're here," Grandfather an-nounced as he pulled the station wagon up to the big house — a two-story white build-ing with green shutters and a wide wrap-around porch.

Benny was the first one out of the car, with Watch at his heels.

"Well, hello, old friend," a deep voice boomed behind them.

Grandfather turned around and ran to greet an elderly man with silvery hair, rosy cheeks, and bright blue eyes. "I saw you drive up from the barn," the man said. "I don't move as fast as I used to, or I would have been up here to greet you before you got out of the car."

Grandfather laughed and shook his head. "You certainly haven't changed, Seymour. It sure is good to see you."

"And these must be your grandchildren," Seymour said.

Grandfather nodded and proudly introduced Henry, Jessie, Violet, Benny, and Watch, who all shook the farmer's hand (including Watch!).

Though frail-looking, Mr. Curtis had a very firm handshake. "Please call me Seymour," the farmer insisted. "None of that Mr. Curtis nonsense. Your grandfather and I have known each other since we were six years old."

"We met in first grade," Grandfather explained as he followed his friend up to the house.

The Aldens entered a small living room with a low ceiling and a worn wooden floor, covered with a small Oriental rug.

"This way," said Seymour, gesturing toward the big kitchen where his wife, Rose, was at the stove stirring a big pot of stew.

Already seated at the long wooden table in front of the stove were two middle-aged men.

"These are my farmhands," Seymour said

as he introduced them to the Aldens. "Mike Johnson and Jeff Wilson have been working for me ever since they were in high school." They were both tall, big-boned men with dark curly hair and blue eyes. Henry noticed Mike had especially large feet, and he wore thick hiking boots. Jeff wore a pair of worn red sneakers. The two men looked a lot alike. The Aldens were not surprised to learn they were cousins.

"Will you be here long?" Jeff asked. Jeff had a wide smile and large white teeth.

"The Aldens are welcome to stay as long as they like," Seymour said. "Goodness knows, I've been trying to get my old friend up here for years now, but he's always been too busy."

Grandfather laughed. "We'll probably stay a week or two," he answered.

"Well, we'll have to put you to work," Jeff said, addressing Henry as he spoke. "We could show you around the farm, and you could help us bale some hay, if you feel like working."

"I could help, too," said Benny.

"Nah, you'd just be in the way," Mike muttered. Benny just stared at the farmhand, too hurt and surprised to say anything more. The others didn't seem to have heard Mike's comment.

"Lunch is ready," Rose announced as she pulled a big tray of warm biscuits out of the oven.

"Oh, homemade buttermilk biscuits. My favorite," said Grandfather, rubbing his hands together. "Did I ever tell you that Rose makes the best biscuits in New England?" he asked his grandchildren.

"Now, James," Rose protested, laughing, "that's an exaggeration." But she looked pleased.

"Everything smells wonderful," said Jessie.

"Food's always good here," Jeff agreed as he heaped stew on his plate. "It keeps Mike and me working here."

"We had a mighty good harvest this year," Mike was telling Grandfather. "Especially with the Baldwins."

"The Northern Spy did well, too," Seymour added.

Benny perked up. "There's an apple called Northern Spy?"

"There sure is, son. You'll have to taste one before you leave," Seymour answered.

"Sure, I'll taste almost anything," Benny said.

"So the orchard is doing very well, Seymour," Grandfather remarked.

"Yes, the orchard is," Seymour said slowly, "but we've been having some other troubles." At this point he exchanged a look with his wife, who was frowning.

"I have to tell them, Rose," Seymour said. "James is one of my best friends."

"But they only just arrived," Rose protested.

"What is this all about?" asked Jeff. By now, everyone at the table was looking at Seymour, who was shaking his head sadly.

"Well, the truth is," Seymour began, choosing his words carefully, "we're being robbed."

"No!" Jeff exclaimed, while Mike whistled under his breath.

CHAPTER 3

The Missing Letters

"You mean someone is stealing your fruit?" Benny asked.

Seymour actually smiled. "No, nothing like that." He cleared his throat. "The fact is, someone is stealing our antiques — not the furniture, but smaller things like my stamp collection and some old family letters."

"Oh, no, Seymour," Grandfather said. "Your stamp collection was very valuable."

Seymour put down his fork. "It was," he agreed. "And so were some of those letters

— at least to me. A lot of them dated from the Civil War."

"Were there any letters from the ghost?" asked Benny.

Seymour looked puzzled, but only for a moment. "Oh, you mean Joshua," he said, chuckling a little. "I see your grandfather has told you all the family history."

"Everyone for miles around knows about Joshua's ghost," Mike reminded the farmer.

"I suppose they do," Seymour agreed as he stirred his coffee. "But to answer your question, Benny, yes, some letters from Joshua were taken, along with Gideon's diary. Gideon was one of my ancestors, the one who built this farm," the farmer added, looking at the Aldens.

"Oh, we know about Gideon," Benny said.

Seymour looked at Grandfather and raised his eyebrows. "I can see you prepared your grandchildren well for this visit," he said.

"But we should be glad you didn't lose all of Gideon's letters," Rose reminded her husband as she handed him a piece of homemade apple pie for dessert.

"No, I have a few left. There are plenty of old letters in this house, some I haven't even read yet," Seymour remarked.

"Seymour, why didn't you tell us about this? When did these robberies take place?" Jeff wanted to know.

Seymour looked at his farmhand. "I didn't notice the missing letters until last night," he said. "And as for the stamp collection, well, I think it disappeared maybe a week ago."

"You should have told us," Jeff persisted.

Seymour looked down at his hands. "Well, the truth is, I, uh, had to make sure those things really were missing. You know how forgetful I can be in my old age."

Jeff nodded, but he looked troubled. "Did you call the police?" he asked.

"I did. They came over to check things out."

"They told us there had been some other robberies nearby, in Chassell," Rose said. "Chassell is the nearest big town," she explained to the Aldens. "The thieves only took small items — old photographs, paintings, antique jewelry, things like that."

"So these thieves want antiques," Jeff said.

"Apparently so." Seymour sounded grim. "I just worry they'll take some of the old swords. But I think they're safe enough in the secret passageway."

"Are you sure?" Jeff asked, looking doubtful. "Everyone who's ever worked on the farm knows about the secret passageway. I wouldn't be surprised if most of the town knew about it, too."

"That's true," said Seymour, frowning. "But only the farm workers and some of my relatives know how to get inside it."

Benny perked up. "You mean the passageway has a secret entrance?"

Seymour nodded. "It has two secret entrances in fact."

"And all the people who work on the farm know how to get inside the passageway?" Henry asked.

"Yes, they would," Seymour answered.

"The only other people who know are my children and grandchildren, and they're sworn to secrecy. The entrance to the passageway has always been a farm secret."

"I guess you can't be too careful," said Jeff as he rose from his seat to stretch his arms. "I'm really sorry this happened, Seymour. Let me know if there's anything I can do to help."

"I will, Jeff, thank you."

"Well, Mike and I should be getting back to work. There's still a lot of clearing and pruning to do."

Mike looked at his hands. He had grown even more quiet during dessert and seemed very upset about the robberies. At last he sighed and rose, thanking the Curtises for lunch.

"Oh, you're welcome, Mike," Rose said.

Mike merely nodded and followed Jeff out the door.

Seymour watched them leave, stirring his coffee. He waited until the farmhands were out of sight before turning to the Aldens.

"You know, I have something to confess,"

Seymour began as Rose cleared the plates from the table with Violet and Benny's help. "This isn't easy for me to say, but the reason I didn't tell Jeff and Mike about these robberies right away is that, well, I just don't know what to think."

"What do you mean?" Grandfather asked.

Seymour sighed and looked close to tears. "Well, it's just that whoever did those robberies knows a lot about me and where I keep my things. I just can't help thinking that the burglar is someone I know pretty well."

"But, Seymour, surely you don't suspect Jeff and Mike. They've been working for you for years, ever since they were boys," Rose said.

"No, I don't believe it could be them, but I do employ other farmhands to help during the picking season."

"Who?" Jessie wanted to know.

"Well, this fall I had two high school students, Veronica and Martin. You'll meet them while you're here — they still help me out around the farm. They're good kids. I know their parents and grandparents."

"You know, Seymour, it's entirely possible this robbery is tied to the other antique robberies in town. It may not be anyone we know at all," Rose said.

"I wish I could believe that." Seymour sounded sad. "I hate to be in the position of suspecting everyone who works around here. But that stamp collection was in a secret drawer in my desk. And nothing else was touched. The thief knew just where to look."

"You've told your farmhands about your secret drawer?" Grandfather asked.

"Well, yes. I like to show that old desk to the people who come in. And Jeff and Mike have seen my stamp collection."

"Did the others know where your stamp collection was?" Jessie asked as she handed Benny more dishes to take off the table.

Seymour scratched his head. "Well, I told Veronica about it. She collects stamps, too."

"I don't think we should jump to any conclusions until we have more evidence,"

Rose suggested. "You know that's what the police said."

"Right," said Seymour. "My wife is the down-to-earth one," he told the Aldens. "She always talks good sense." The farmer rose slowly. "Who would like to take a walk around the farm?" he asked.

"Me." Benny was the first to answer. "Can we see the secret passageway, too?"

"Follow me," Seymour said, walking toward the door.

"Oh, Seymour, before you go, why don't you show the Aldens where their rooms are. They may want to unpack, or at least unload their belongings from the car. They've only just arrived."

"Good idea," said Seymour. "I told you Rose is the sensible one."

Everyone laughed.

The bedrooms were all upstairs on the second floor. Jessie and Violet had a fireplace and a four-poster bed in their room. Henry and Benny shared a corner room with built-in beds and bookcases.

"This is like a ship's cabin," Henry said happily when he saw it.

The Aldens unpacked quickly, and before long they were following Seymour outside toward the barn.

On the way, they passed a long vegetable garden guarded by a scarecrow made from sticks and straw. He wore a flannel shirt, loose denim pants, and a black felt hat.

"This is a great scarecrow," Benny remarked.

Seymour chuckled. "He sure comes in handy in the summer when he keeps the crows from eating all our vegetables."

One side of the old red barn was filled with hay and the other had stalls for two horses, three cows, and a goat named Elvira.

"You watch out for Elvira," the farmer warned the Aldens. "She'll eat anything in sight, even the shirt off your back, if you're not careful."

Benny giggled.

"I'm serious," Seymour said. "She's been known to nibble on laundry that's hanging outside to dry. And she eats everyone's food." Seymour shook his head and gave Elvira a playful pat.

"How often do you feed the animals?" Jessie wanted to know.

"Twice a day, now that winter's coming on," the farmer answered. "Early in the morning, and then again in the late afternoon. And sometimes they also get snacks during the day." Seymour reached into his pocket for two cubes of sugar, which he handed to Benny.

"Here, son, you can give these to the horses. They're outside," Seymour said, leading the way out to the pasture.

Once outside, Benny walked over to look at the two horses who were grazing near the fence. "They don't bite, do they?" Benny wanted to know.

"Nah, they're tame as can be," the farmer assured him. The horses moved closer to Benny, and Benny promptly took a few steps backward, away from the fence.

"No need to be afraid," Seymour said. He reached through the fence to pat the white horse on the nose. "This one is called Hazel," he told the Aldens.

"Hazel?" Violet asked, a little puzzled.

"Her eyes are hazel," the farmer answered.

"And this one here" — Seymour pointed to her gray companion — "is Mister Mist."

Violet put her hand through the fence to stroke Mister Mist's mane.

"Now, Benny, if you want to feed Hazel, put the sugar on the palm of your hand and hold your hand flat."

Benny followed the farmer's instructions. "Oooh, she tickles," said Benny, yanking his hand away after the horse had taken the sugar cube. Then he quickly gave Mister Mist his sugar, while Seymour gently nudged Hazel out of the way.

Benny did not want to leave the horses, but the others were eager to continue exploring the farm.

Seymour led the way to a long, low building. "This is a shed and junk room," the farmer explained as he pulled open the wooden door and held it for the Aldens.

"Wow!" Henry exclaimed when his eyes had adjusted to the dim light.

Inside was a large wagon. It was old and rusted now, but Seymour told them it had been used as a horse-drawn buggy. The wagon was piled high with old trunks, bundles of yellowed newspapers, and wooden crates filled with glass jars and old rusty tools.

Half the shed held modern farm equipment: tractors, ladders, buckets, hoses, pitchforks, fertilizers, and pesticides. But it was the buggy that interested the Aldens the most.

"How old is it?" Henry wanted to know.

"What's in all those trunks?" asked Benny.

"One question at a time," Seymour advised, laughing. "That buggy dates back to Gideon's time, I dare say. As for what's in those trunks, I suggest that some rainy day you all have a look."

"Oh, we'd love to do that," Jessie answered for all of them.

"I've rummaged around in one or two of them," Seymour continued. "As far as I can recall, I found some old clothes, some hats, and even some books. Just about all the Curtises are collectors. We never seem to throw anything away."

"Is the secret passageway in this shed?" Benny wanted to know.

"Ah, young man, I was saving the best part for last," Seymour said. "We need to go back up to the house to find the secret passageway."

"Okay," said Benny, racing outside.

Once in the house, Seymour led the Aldens downstairs to the basement — a long, low room with stone walls and a dirt floor.

The children looked all around the basement. The only door in any of the walls was one at the top of a short wooden staircase that obviously led to the outside.

"How can there be a secret door?" Henry

asked. "It would have to be made out of this stone that's in the walls, and that would be awfully heavy."

Violet spotted a tall wooden cabinet that stood against one wall near a corner. "Is the door behind this cabinet?" she asked.

Seymour chuckled. "You're pretty darn close!" he answered as he walked over to the cabinet and opened it. There was little inside it besides two flashlights and an old kerosene lamp on the top shelf.

Seymour moved the lamp aside, handed one flashlight to Henry, and switched on the other. Holding it in one hand, he took hold of one shelf, jiggled it slightly, then pushed on it.

To the Aldens' amazement, all the shelves and the back of the cabinet swung backward like a door, revealing a narrow opening. A cold draft blew out at them.

"The secret passageway!" shouted Benny.

CHAPTER 4

The Secret Passageway

The Aldens peered inside the opening. The passageway looked so dark and spooky with cobwebs hanging overhead that Benny was suddenly afraid to step inside, even after Seymour handed him a flashlight.

"Come on, Benny. This is one of the things you came all this way to see," Seymour said.

"I'll go after Henry," Benny said in a quavery voice.

Henry had to bend down to go through

the opening. He shone his flashlight against the walls and gave a gasp.

"What's the matter?" asked Benny, who was right behind his brother.

"It's a . . . it's just that I thought I saw a person in here," Henry explained, sounding a little sheepish. "Now I see that it's a suit of armor." Henry shone his flashlight all around. He saw not just one but six steel suits of armor, complete with helmets, lining the walls of the narrow passageway.

"Neat," Benny said as he came inside. The others crowded in behind him.

Besides the armor, there were lots of old weapons: knights' swords, a battle-ax, a crossbow, and two big shields.

"Wow!" said Benny. "Did they really fight with all this stuff?"

"No, Benny," said Seymour with a chuckle. "For one thing, not all of it is real equipment from the Middle Ages. This suit, for example, is stage armor. It was used in a play in Boston many years ago. It looks real, but it's much lighter than the other suits."

"Are these swords all real?" asked Henry.

"Yes, Henry, they are indeed. This one is from the fifteenth century," the farmer said, shining his light on it. "And this curved one is from Turkey, and here is a naval cutlass from Colonial times here in America." Seymour beamed the flashlight on a short, heavy, curved sword. Then Seymour looked around the passageway and said nothing more for a few moments.

"Is something the matter?" Jessie asked.

"It's strange, but I can't find Gideon's officer's saber from the Civil War. It was down here the last time I was."

Jessie and Henry exchanged glances. "You don't think it was stolen, do you?" Henry asked.

The farmer scratched his head. "I don't know what to think. I'd find it hard to believe a burglar would know how to get inside this secret passageway. It's too well hidden. It was built before the Civil War to help runaway slaves escape north. After the Civil War, my ancestor, Gideon, used this passageway to store his sword and armor collection. His collection has been down here ever since, pretty much just the way you see it, though my children and grand-children have sometimes borrowed some of the armor to use as Halloween costumes."

"Maybe someone borrowed that Civil War sword for a costume," Jessie suggested hopefully.

Seymour sighed. "I hope so. I must ask Rose if she knows anything about it."

Violet shone her flashlight on the dirt floor to look for clues. But there weren't any, just lots of indistinguishable footprints.

By now the Aldens and Seymour were at the end of the passageway. Seymour shone his light on the wooden trapdoor above them. "That door goes right into the barn," he said. "When we go through it, we'll be right next to Elvira's stall."

Jessie giggled. "Won't she be surprised."

Seymour fetched the ladder that was rest-ing behind one of the suits of armor.

"Want to go out this way?" he asked.

"Sure, why not," Jessie answered for all of them.

Henry was the first one up the ladder.

"Just push the door out," Seymour advised Henry.

"It's heavy," Henry answered, panting.

"I know," said Seymour. "It's part of the floor. I never go out this way because I'm getting too old to fool with that heavy trapdoor."

"I know what you mean," Henry said, huffing. "Aha, finally it's out!" Henry climbed out into the barn. Elvira came over to greet him.

"Your goat is here, Jessie," Henry called into the passageway.

When they were all in the barn, Seymour lowered the trapdoor, then scattered straw to conceal it. Then the Aldens insisted on helping Seymour with the animals. They brought the horses in from the pasture and fed them oats. The cows got hay that Henry pitched into their stall.

The sun was low in the sky when the Aldens walked back to the house with Seymour. Flocks of geese flew overhead, forming a pattern that looked like the letter V.

As soon as they were in the house, Seymour and the Aldens lost no time asking Rose if she had seen Gideon's sword.

"No, I haven't," Rose said, wiping her hands on her blue-and-white-checked apron. "I haven't been in that passageway in months."

"Neither have I." Seymour was scratching his head. He sighed heavily. "You don't know of anyone borrowing that sword for a Halloween costume, or some such getup?"

Rose frowned. "Well, no. I don't remember telling anyone they could borrow a costume this year."

The Aldens looked at one another. "Do you think someone might have borrowed that sword without telling you?" Jessie asked gently.

Seymour sighed and looked at his wife. "It's possible," he said, almost as if he were trying to convince himself. "I mean, we certainly don't keep things under lock and key here. We've never had to."

"That's true," Rose agreed. "We've never had to — until now."

CHAPTER 5

Veronica

That evening, after an early dinner, the four Alden children met in Jessie and Violet's room.

"We just have to help Seymour and Rose solve this mystery," Violet was saying as she leaned back against two of the lacy white pillows piled on the bed.

"All this is very upsetting for them," Henry agreed, "especially since they think the burglar may be someone who works for them."

"I hope it's not," Violet said.

"I hope not, too," said Henry. "But a burglar who works here would be easier to catch."

"True," Jessie agreed. She pulled a notebook and pencil out of her blue duffel bag. "We should make a list of all the people who work on this farm and who know about the entrances to the passageway."

"Well, there's Jeff and Mike," Violet said, "the ones we met at lunch."

"The ones who've been working on the farm since they were in high school." Jessie was busy scribbling in her notebook.

"Mike seemed awfully quiet once the robberies were mentioned," Violet remarked.

"I don't think Mike and Jeff are really suspects," Henry said.

"What makes you so sure?" Jessie said, holding her pencil poised over her notebook.

"Seymour has known them too long, and nothing has ever been taken from the farm before," Henry answered.

"That's true." Jessie tapped her pencil on her notepad.

"Well, that leaves Veronica and Martin, the two high school kids who just started working on the farm this year," Violet said.

"The ones we haven't seen yet," Jessie said, looking up from her notebook.

"We should ask Seymour if we can meet them tomorrow," Henry said.

"And we should also try to find Benny's ghost. Right, Benny?" Jessie looked over at her brother, only to find that Benny had fallen sound asleep and was snoring gently.

"It's been a long day," Jessie whispered.

Henry nodded as he carefully picked up Benny to carry him off to bed.

The next morning the Aldens woke up just before sunrise. "It was the rooster," Benny told Grandfather at breakfast. "It was the rooster that got me up so early."

"That's his job," Grandfather said, laughing.

As soon as breakfast was over, Henry,

Jessie, Violet, and Benny hurried to the barn to help Seymour feed the animals.

They watched carefully as Seymour milked the cows. "I do it the old-fashioned way," he said as he sat on a pail beside one of his cows and began pulling at her teats. Milk squirted into another pail under the cow.

"Many farmers use milking machines now," Seymour explained. "But I don't have enough cows for a machine. It's easier for me to milk them this way."

"I'd like to try to milk a cow before I leave," Henry said.

"Oh, I trust you'll have the chance," said Seymour, chuckling. "But right now, if you like, you can brush down the horses."

"Sure," said Henry, grabbing a brush.

"Hey, that's my job." A tall, thin girl with shiny brown hair tied back in a ponytail strode into the barn. "I always brush the horses," she said haughtily. "They're used to me." The girl wore blue jeans, a red-and-black-plaid wool jacket, riding boots, and a red bandanna around her neck. Her blue eyes flashed as she glared at Henry.

"Now, Veronica," Seymour said gently. "It's good for the horses to have other folks brushing them down once in a while. They need to get used to other people."

Veronica continued to glare at the Aldens as Seymour introduced them to her.

"Are you used to horses?" she asked Henry, who was still holding the brush. "Do you know how to groom them properly?"

"Well, not really," Henry was forced to admit.

Veronica rolled her eyes.

"That's all right, son," said Seymour. "Veronica or I can teach you all you need to know. Isn't that right, Veronica?"

Veronica sighed heavily. "How long will you be staying here?" she asked.

"About a week or two," Jessie answered for all of them.

"Well, that's hardly worth taking the time to teach you," Veronica remarked.

"Now, Veronica," Seymour spoke sharply, "the Aldens are my guests. They've already been a big help to me, and I will thank you to treat them politely. If you don't feel like showing them what needs to be done, then I'll teach them myself."

Veronica scowled. "I'll show them," she said sullenly.

Veronica and the Aldens spent the next hour together feeding, grooming, and brushing the horses, while Seymour mended some fences outside. Veronica showed the Aldens what had to be done by doing most of the work herself, while they watched.

"Now, I don't want you riding Hazel or Mister Mist without my permission," Veronica was saying as she brushed Mister Mist. "They're not used to strangers. They only like it when I handle them. Seymour says I'm the best rider on this farm — the best rider in this whole town, in fact."

"We wouldn't ride them without asking anyone," Jessie said.

"Good."

Henry cleared his throat. "It's a shame about those robberies, isn't it?"

Veronica stiffened. "What robberies are you talking about?"

"You know, the robberies on this farm," Jessie said. "Someone stole Seymour's stamp collection and some old letters written more than a hundred years ago."

Veronica frowned. "No one told me," she said. "When did this happen?"

"A few days ago," Henry answered. "At least that's when Seymour noticed that the stamp collection and letters were missing."

"He's missing a sword, too. A sword from the Civil War," Benny added before he noticed Jessie's face warning him to keep quiet.

Veronica looked puzzled. "You mean someone stole a sword out of that musty old passageway?"

Henry nodded.

"I don't like to hear that there were burglars near the barn because that means the horses could be in danger," Veronica said as she fluffed up Mister Mist's mane.

"From what Seymour said, these burglars are after antiques, not animals," Henry pointed out.

"Well, still, I worry. If anything happened

to these horses, I don't know what I'd do."

"You seem to care for these horses very much," Violet said, softening a little toward Veronica.

"Well, of course. Who wouldn't?" Veronica exclaimed. Then she frowned suddenly and turned away from the Aldens to hang the grooming brushes back on the wall. "I have to go home now. I mostly just help with the horses now that the picking season is over."

"Have you been working here long?" Henry wanted to know.

"Have you been here long enough to see the ghost?" Benny asked.

"No and no." Veronica actually smiled for the first time that morning. "I began working for Seymour this fall because he needed the extra help, but I've known Rose and Seymour all my life, practically. I live just down the road."

"Why have you never seen the ghost if you live near here?" Benny asked.

"Well, to tell you the truth," Veronica began in a superior tone of voice, "I don't believe in ghosts. Maybe that's why I've never seen it." With that, Veronica spun around and walked out of the barn before the Aldens could say anything more.

"Boy, is she rude," Jessie muttered.

"She wasn't so bad, once we got her to talk more," Violet remarked.

"But she's such a show-off." Jessie was almost sputtering. "She hardly let us touch her precious horses, and they're not even her horses, really. And did you see the way she acted when we mentioned those robberies?"

"Yeah, she looked kind of uncomfortable. And then she told us she'd never heard about them," Henry said.

"We'll have to watch her," Jessie said.

"We should watch everybody," Henry advised.

"Now, don't you mind Veronica too much," Seymour told the Aldens when he walked back into the barn. "She acts all high and mighty, especially when it comes to the horses, but she's all right."

Jessie was not convinced.

"Seymour?" Benny began. "You believe in the ghost, don't you?"

"Benny, to tell you the truth, I've never actually seen it. But people have noticed signs."

"What kind of signs?" Benny sounded eager.

Seymour chose his words carefully. "Well, Benny, some of the farm workers say they've heard things."

Benny nodded. "Grandfather told us about that," he said.

"And some say they've actually seen markings on the trunks of the apple trees. Markings carved by a knife of some sort," Seymour continued. "They think those markings are the work of the ghost because no one else would mark those trees up."

Benny's eyes were very round.

"Do you believe a ghost made those markings?" Violet asked.

Seymour's eyes twinkled. "Well, now that you mention it, there is another explanation for these markings," he answered.

"There is?" Benny couldn't believe it.

Seymour nodded. "When my children were little, they used to make carvings in those trees with their penknives. But when I caught them doing that, I made them stop."

"So, those markings are pretty old, then," Henry remarked.

"Yes, most of them are, but Jeff told me he's been seeing some new ones. He thinks it's the work of kids in the neighborhood."

"It could be the work of the ghost," Benny said firmly.

"Could be," Seymour said. "That's what a lot of people think."

"This we have to see!" Henry exclaimed.

CHAPTER 6

Signs in the Orchard

Before long, the Aldens were walking through thick rows of apple trees. The wind swirled red and yellow leaves around them.

"It's pretty here," Violet observed.

"It is," Benny agreed. "But how are we ever going to hear the ghost with all this wind?"

Henry shook his head and stopped before a group of apple trees with thicker trunks. "These look like the oldest trees in the orchard," he said. "I think this is where Seymour said some markings would be."

Indeed, when the Aldens bent down they could see weathered drawings carved into the bark. There was an *X*, an *O*, and a symbol that Henry thought looked like a rough drawing of a sword.

"Maybe the *O* is really an apple," Violet suggested.

"What does the *X* stand for?" Benny wanted to know.

Henry shrugged. "Beats me," he said. "Remember, this was part of a game Seymour's children used to play."

"Let's see if we can't find the newer markings," Jessie suggested. "These carvings are pretty faded."

The Aldens walked alongside the trees, crunching fallen leaves beneath their sneakers. Benny gathered a pile of the leaves in his arms and threw them at Violet. Violet threw some leaves back at Benny. Before long, masses of leaves whirled through the air.

"Looks like you're having fun," a voice said.

The Aldens turned to face a tall blond

boy who stood grinning at them. "I was just pruning some of these apple trees," the boy explained as he pointed to the large power saw by his feet. "I work in this orchard part-time after school."

"Are you Martin?" Jessie asked.

The boy nodded. "I am," he said. "And you must be the Aldens. Seymour told me you'd be visiting. I'm pleased to meet you."

"We're pleased to meet you, too," Jessie said for all of them.

"We're looking at these markings on the tree trunks," Benny informed Martin. "Do you know about them?"

"Oh, those," Martin said, laughing. "I think they must have been part of a game the Curtis children used to play."

Benny looked disappointed.

"Are there any other markings like this?" Violet asked.

"I haven't seen any," Martin answered. "But then again, I haven't been looking."

"What do you know about the ghost?" Benny asked Martin.

Martin laughed. "Well, I've heard some

rustling in the trees, but I think it's the sound of an animal, not a ghost."

"You've never seen the ghost?" Benny asked.

"No, I don't think I have," Martin answered. "But you know, in most of the ghost stories I've read, the ghost never actually appears."

"It doesn't?" Benny's eyes were as round as saucers.

"No." Martin sounded very sure. "The room, or the area where the ghost is supposed to appear, just gets colder. And lights flicker, that kind of stuff. People sense a ghost is around, but no one ever actually sees it."

"I never thought of it that way." Benny sounded much happier. He walked farther into the orchard, and the others followed, including Martin.

Henry was the first to see two markings scratched into the bark of one tree. "These markings look newer!" he exclaimed.

"Why do you think so?" Violet asked as she bent down to look at them more carefully.

"They don't look as weathered," Henry answered. "So it's easier to make out what they are."

"It's true," Jessie agreed. She sat on the ground near Henry. "Here's a drawing of a sword with a curved blade."

"That's interesting," Henry said. "Do you think this is still part of the game?"

"It could be a message or signal for someone," Violet suggested.

Jessie's eyes lit up. "I wonder if the sword that's missing has a curved blade."

"Maybe it's the ghost of Joshua saying he wants that sword," Benny pointed out.

"Maybe," Martin said. "But I'll bet it's a signal for someone who's alive today, maybe the burglars who take antiques." He sounded as excited as Jessie.

"Yes," Henry agreed. "The message could be that the coast is clear to take a sword with a curved blade."

"We should tell Seymour right away," Jessie said. Benny had already turned around to go back to the farmhouse.

The Aldens and Martin had not gotten

too far when Veronica stepped out from behind a tree and walked directly into their path.

"Martin, I've been looking all over for you." She sounded angry.

"Oh, hi, Veronica," Martin said, blushing a little.

"Why weren't you over by the tree where you said you would be? Do you know how long it's taken me to find you?"

"Well, Veronica, I —"

Veronica put her hands on her hips. "I'm sure you have a good excuse, as always," she interrupted.

"Veronica, I was helping the Aldens find some markings on the trees. We think these markings might be a clue — you know, for those burglaries."

"Oh." Veronica looked somewhat interested. "Why don't we take a walk and you can tell me all about it," Veronica suggested, locking her arm through Martin's.

"So long," Martin said, nodding to the Aldens. He looked sorry to be saying goodbye to them. Veronica firmly led Martin away without a word to the Aldens.

"I can't believe someone as nice as Martin is going out with Veronica," Jessie muttered as the four walked quickly in the other direction — toward the farmhouse.

"She is so rude to us," Violet complained. "Did you see how she acted like we weren't even there?"

"She probably wishes we weren't around," Jessie remarked. "If it weren't for us, Martin would have been waiting for her by the tree."

"Yeah," Benny agreed.

"You know," Henry began, "I wonder how much of our conversation she overheard. I wonder how long she was behind that tree."

"Do you think she might have been spying on us?" Violet wondered.

"That is just what I was thinking," Henry admitted.

"Well, did you see the markings?" Seymour wanted to know as soon as the Aldens walked in the door of the farmhouse.

"We sure did," Jessie said.

"We saw two kinds," Benny added. "Old ones and new ones. And I bet the new ones were drawn by the ghost."

"Where were these new markings, exactly?" Seymour wanted to know.

"Near the horse's pasture," Violet answered.

"We saw a drawing of a sword with a curved blade on one of the trees. It didn't look as old and faded as the others," Henry explained.

"That's odd," Seymour said, scratching his chin. "The missing sword has a curved blade."

"We thought it might," Henry said, looking excited. "We think it might be a signal."

"A signal for the burglar," Seymour said, frowning. "I'd like to see this marking."

"We'll lead the way," Henry said.

Before Seymour and the Aldens could get out the door, they heard Grandfather calling them from the living room. "Look at this!" Grandfather was almost shouting. The Aldens rushed into the living room ahead of Seymour.

They found their grandfather seated in an old armchair by the window, rustling the newspaper, which lay open on his lap.

"Take a look at this story," Grandfather said as he handed the paper to Henry.

" 'Memories of Yesteryear.' " Henry read the headline aloud while the others peered over his shoulder — all but Benny, who was too short.

" 'Today's column features a letter that has much to tell us about what life was like in Chassell in the horse-and-buggy days,' " Henry continued reading. Then he gasped.

"What, what's the matter?" Benny cried.

"This letter is addressed to Joshua Curtis," Henry said, lowering the paper so Benny could see it.

"Wow, it was written in 1857," Violet said, looking over Benny's shoulder.

Seymour put on his spectacles and took a closer look at the paper. "Just as I thought," he said grimly. "That's one of Gideon's letters to Joshua. It's also one of the letters that was stolen from my desk."

Henry looked puzzled. "Why did Gideon have a letter addressed to Joshua? Wouldn't Joshua have that letter?"

"Good question," Seymour said. "Gideon made copies of every letter he sent. That's why there's so much correspondence in this house."

"I can't believe that's one of the stolen letters!" Rose said.

"It is," Seymour said, a little gruffly. "It's the letter where Gideon is inviting Joshua to come up for a visit."

"I don't think I ever read that letter," Rose said slowly.

"James, why don't you read that letter aloud?" Seymour suggested.

Grandfather cleared his throat and read:

15 October 1857

Dear Cousin Joshua,
 I regret to have taken so long to answer your letter dated August third. We have been busy here planting & gathering this

year's crop of apples & corn. It is hard to believe that winter approaches as it has been very warm this October.

Sybil is preparing for the winter holidays, & we are hoping you may join us. I know the trip from Virginia is long, but we could arrange to meet you at the train station & bring you to our farm.

I know we must discuss this matter of dividing my father's sword & armor collection. I have now read his will & diary & see that he wanted me to inherit it. We can discuss this further when I see you.

Sybil, the children, & I so hope you can visit & we await your response.

Your cousin, Gideon

"Does the paper say anything about where they found this letter?" Violet asked.

"Yes, it does," Henry answered. "The letter was sent to them by a Mrs. Louise Hathaway, head librarian for the Chassell Public Library."

"I wonder where Louise found that letter," Rose remarked. "We know her. She would never steal anything from anyone."

"We should probably pay a visit to the local library tomorrow," Henry offered. "We can ask her in person."

"Oh, would you?" Seymour sounded grateful. "I can't leave the farm tomorrow because I want to supervise the pruning."

"We'd be glad to go to the library," Jessie said. "Maybe we can find more clues there."

CHAPTER 7

A Stranger in the Library

The Aldens were up early the next morning. They helped feed the animals and ate a quick breakfast. Then they borrowed some old bicycles that were in the shed and rode into Chassell.

The library was in a large white clapboard house that was painted white and had green shutters. The Aldens climbed up the brick staircase and entered a large, comfortable reading room.

Luckily Mrs. Hathaway was one of the librarians on duty. She towered over the

Aldens, even Henry, when she stood.

"We're guests of the Curtises," Henry began, looking up at the librarian, who was staring at him very closely.

"Yes."

"Well, we were curious about the old letter reprinted in the paper. The paper said that was your letter — I mean, that the letter belonged to you."

Mrs. Hathaway nodded.

"We were just wondering where you found that letter. I mean, did you know it was stolen property?" Henry continued.

Mrs. Hathaway scowled. "Now, young man, I bought that letter at a respectable antique shop on the outskirts of town — a shop I am sure would not be selling stolen property."

"But there have been other antiques stolen in town recently," Jessie persisted.

Mrs. Hathaway nodded a bit impatiently. "Yes, young lady, I am aware of that. But I am sure this shop would not be selling stolen goods, as I've said before."

"Did you buy any other letters with it?" Jessie wanted to know.

"No, I did not, not this time, though I have bought old letters and diaries from that shop in the past. I collect articles on the town's early history for the library."

"Are the letters you've bought from this shop in the library?" Jessie asked eagerly.

"They most certainly are. You'll find them on display in the small reading room to the right," said Mrs. Hathaway, pointing. "Now may I ask why you think that letter in the paper was stolen?"

The Aldens looked at one another. "That letter belonged to Mr. Curtis," Benny blurted out. "He's had a bunch of letters and other things stolen from his house."

Mrs. Hathaway looked surprised, even a little embarrassed. "Goodness, I had no idea."

Jessie told Mrs. Hathaway about the robberies on the farm. When she was finished, Mrs. Hathaway shook her head. "Poor Seymour. He certainly has been having trouble. I suppose it makes sense that letter belongs to him, since it does concern one of his ancestors. I must return it to him." Mrs.

Hathaway led the Aldens to the display case and unlocked it.

"Here are the other old letters that belong to the library. Many were donated or purchased a long time ago, so I doubt they belong to Seymour."

Mrs. Hathaway carefully took Joshua's letter out of the display case. "I will go out to the farm myself to return this to Seymour," she told the Aldens. "Please tell him I'll visit tonight when I'm off duty."

Henry nodded. "We'll tell him."

"I must also let the antique store know about this," Mrs. Hathaway said.

"We'd like to talk to this antique dealer, too," Henry said.

"That's probably a good idea," Mrs. Hathaway remarked. "Seymour is indeed lucky to have you as houseguests."

"While we're here," Violet began shyly, "would it be all right if we looked through these other old letters? We would love to read more about Gideon's time." She nodded in the direction of the display case.

"Well, I suppose you could, if you're very

careful with them," the librarian answered, looking suspiciously at Benny.

"We will be," Henry assured her.

With the librarian's permission, the Aldens moved the contents of the display case to a reading table so they could study the old maps and letters more closely.

"Look, here's the Curtis farm," Henry said, pointing at an old map. "They sure had a lot of land in the old days," he said. "Look, they had all the land that now belongs to the Browns — you know, the farm we passed on the way to town."

"That's interesting," Jessie said thoughtfully. "Maybe they had to sell some of their land off because they needed the money."

"Look at this. Here's an old drawing of Chassell in 1890. It looks pretty much the same," Violet remarked as she carefully handed the drawing to Henry.

"Yeah, except you don't see too many horse-drawn carts in the street now," Henry joked. "Also, the streets weren't paved then."

"Here's a picture of the old library when

it was a house with a family in it." Violet handed the yellowed photograph to Jessie.

"Look, there are some Curtises in the picture," Violet said, pointing at the caption.

The Aldens were so intent on their research, none of them noticed the tall man with blond hair and a beard who approached their table. He had been listening to their conversation ever since they had begun talking to the librarian. Finally he cleared his throat.

Violet looked up, startled. "Pardon me," the man said. "I'm Blake Ambrose."

The Aldens nodded politely. The name was not familiar to them.

"I'm the author of numerous mysteries and horror stories," the man continued, looking a little disappointed that the Aldens had never heard of him. "My newest book is set in a small nineteenth-century New England village, much like Chassell."

The Aldens nodded politely. "Is that why you're in this library?" Benny wanted to know.

"Well, yes," the author answered. He acted as if Benny had asked a very stupid question. "I'm doing some research on this town. And I, uh, couldn't help overhearing your earlier conversation with Mrs. Hathaway. I could perhaps help you in your research. You see, I am an expert on early American history." Mr. Ambrose stood up very straight as he said this.

Jessie looked at him a little suspiciously but did not say anything.

"How long have you been staying with the Curtises?" Mr. Ambrose wanted to know.

"Not that long," Violet answered vaguely. "Do you know them?"

"The Curtises are an old New England family. I've been reading about them here. Are you going to be staying out at their orchard a long time?"

"A couple of weeks," Henry answered.

"Have you discovered any skeletons in the closet?" the author joked.

"What?" Benny looked puzzled.

"You know, old family secrets."

"Well, we're trying to find out more about what life was like in the ghost's time," Benny answered, not noticing Jessie's warning look.

"Oh, you mean Joshua," the author replied with a wink.

"You know about Joshua?" Jessie sounded surprised.

"I certainly do," the author replied. "The story of Joshua and his disappearance is an interesting part of the history of this town."

"Do you know what happened to Joshua?" Benny asked.

"I'm working on finding out," the author replied.

"We are, too," Benny said, looking at the stack of yellowed letters on the desk in front of him. "And so far we haven't had much luck."

"We'll let you know if we have any questions about anything," Henry told Mr. Ambrose, who was peering at a letter over Henry's shoulder.

"Good day," the author said as he walked away.

"Maybe we should have been a little friendlier to him," Violet whispered when the author had disappeared into the reference section.

"I think he was kind of nosy," Henry said. "I didn't like him looking over my shoulder like that."

"Yeah, I didn't really trust him, either," Jessie said. "That's why I didn't want you telling him too much, Benny."

"I don't think I told him anything he didn't know already," Benny pointed out.

"I don't think you did," Jessie said reassuringly.

"He may have only been trying to help us," Violet said as she pulled her hair back into a ponytail and fastened it with a lavender ribbon.

Henry shrugged. "It sounds like he spends a lot of time in the library. If we have any questions, we know where to find him."

The Aldens spent the rest of the morning reading old letters and looking at maps and photographs, but they could find no further clues to the mystery of Joshua's disappearance.

"We'd better go to the antique store soon," Henry said finally, looking at his watch. "It's going to take us a while to get there."

"Can't we have lunch first?" Benny suggested. "I'm starving."

"Good idea," Jessie said approvingly.

Before they left, Mrs. Hathaway gave the Aldens detailed directions on how to find the antique store. "It's really a barn with a lot of old furniture and other odds and ends in it," she said. "And it's just a little ways outside of Chassell on Old Post Road, the road you took from Seymour's farm. You can't miss it."

"Do you know where we might go for lunch?" Jessie asked as the Aldens were on their way out the door.

"The Doughnut Shop across the street sells delicious sandwiches as well as home-made pies, cakes, and, of course, doughnuts."

"Let's go!" Benny almost shouted.

* * *

When the Aldens entered the Doughnut Shop, they saw Blake Ambrose seated at a table reading a newspaper.

"That's funny. I never saw him leave the library," Henry remarked.

Jessie shrugged. "We weren't looking at the door the whole time," she reminded Henry.

The author looked up and waved as a waitress led the Aldens past his table, but he seemed too absorbed in his newspaper to want to talk.

"Let's not take too long with lunch," Henry warned as the Aldens sat in a booth by the window. "We want to have plenty of time at the antique shop and still get home before dark."

"Can't we at least have dessert?" Benny pleaded, eyeing a plate of homemade chocolate doughnuts behind the counter.

"Why don't we have lunch here and then take some doughnuts to go," Jessie suggested.

"Okay," Benny reluctantly agreed.

While the Aldens were wolfing down their bacon, lettuce, and tomato sandwiches, Martin and Veronica walked into the Doughnut Shop. Martin smiled and waved to the Aldens, but Veronica ignored them. To their surprise, Veronica did wave to Blake Ambrose, who nodded and smiled at her.

"How do they know each other?" Henry wondered.

"Yeah, that's strange," Jessie agreed. "Maybe we can ask Martin." Jessie was about to wave Martin over to their table, but he was busy buying two jelly doughnuts at the counter. He quickly paid for them and walked out of the store with Veronica at his heels.

"Very strange," Violet said. "Maybe we should ask Mr. Ambrose how he knows Veronica."

But when they turned around to look at Blake Ambrose, the author had vanished.

"How did we miss him?" Henry was surprised. "He was just here."

Jessie looked over at the author's table.

The remains of his tuna sandwich lay on his plate. The newspaper he had been reading was neatly folded beside his place setting, and he had left money on the table to pay for his meal.

"He sure comes and goes quickly," Jessie remarked. "I think it's interesting that Veronica knows him. That may be an important clue."

"You mean because Veronica works on the farm?" Violet asked.

Jessie nodded. "Veronica could be giving Blake information about the secret passageway and what's in it."

"That's true," Henry agreed. "But we really don't have any evidence that Blake is involved in these burglaries. All we know is that he's nosy."

"And he knows Veronica," Jessie repeated as she pulled her notebook out of her backpack. She added Blake's name to her list of suspects.

When the Aldens were finished, they paid for their lunch at the counter and bought a bag of assorted doughnuts to go. (Benny made sure they were mostly chocolate ones.) Then they walked back to the library to get their bicycles.

Once on the road, Benny was sure he kept seeing the same large blue car not too far behind them. Henry noticed it, too, and wondered if they were being followed.

By the time the Aldens reached the store, the car had disappeared. They never saw the driver.

CHAPTER 8

The Antique Store

"Goodness, I had no idea that letter was stolen. That's dreadful!" the owner of the antique store exclaimed. Mrs. Holmes was a round, short woman with wiry gray hair. "I would never knowingly sell stolen merchandise," she told the Aldens. "I must call the police about this."

"Mrs. Holmes," Jessie said gently, "do you remember who brought the letter in?"

The owner sighed and looked around her store. "I have so many things in here," she said wearily. "It's hard to keep track of who brings in what. I buy most of my things at yard sales and auctions, but I don't believe that's where the letter came from. I wish I could remember more. I really do. And I must apologize to Seymour." Mrs. Holmes was wringing her hands.

"That letter would have come in recently," Henry pointed out.

"Well, we don't know that for sure," Jessie reminded her brother. "Seymour doesn't exactly know when the letters were stolen."

"True," Henry agreed. "But we think it was within the last month or so."

"Seymour is also missing a stamp collection and a sword dating from the Civil War. You don't have anything like that around, do you?" Henry asked.

Mrs. Holmes shook her head. "Good heavens, no. That I'm sure of. I just wish I could remember more about the letter. If you'll give me a few moments, I'll check my files. Perhaps I can find some record there."

"Sure, we'll just look around your store

awhile," Violet offered. "You might even remember more while we're here."

"I'll certainly try to," Mrs. Holmes assured her. "I just wish I kept better records of things." The owner vanished behind a large oak desk and started rummaging through some cardboard boxes that served as her filing cabinets.

Henry walked over to a pile of newspapers. Jessie looked at some old glass vases in a cabinet. Violet and Benny went to a corner where there were some old toys: dolls, wooden blocks, and rocking horses.

"These are such old toys," Violet said as she lifted a doll's dress to inspect her petticoat.

"Those are the best kind," the owner muttered. She sat on the floor surrounded by scraps of paper. "Oh, this is useless," she said sadly. "I'm never going to find anything in this mess."

Violet came over to her. "Mrs. Holmes," she began, "do you remember buying the letter from someone?"

The owner nodded and pushed her wire-rimmed glasses on top of her head. "I believe I did. I don't remember buying that letter at a yard sale. I think I would have remembered that."

"Was this person who sold you the letter a woman or a man?" Violet continued.

"A man, I believe," Mrs. Holmes answered.

"Did this man have long blond hair and a beard? Did he say he was an author?" Violet asked.

Mrs. Holmes frowned. "No, I don't remember meeting anyone like that. I usually remember faces. That's about all I do remember well."

The Aldens waited while Mrs. Holmes rummaged through a few more cardboard boxes stuffed with papers, but she never found any record of the letter.

"I don't want to keep you here any longer," the owner finally said. "I know Seymour's number. If I find anything, or remember who sold me the letter, I will give you a call, I promise."

"Thanks for all you have done," Jessie said as the Aldens waved good-bye and filed out the door. Once outside, they were surprised to find that the sun was low.

"We should try to get home before dark," Henry warned the others.

"I didn't realize we had been in that store so long," Jessie remarked. "Everything was so old in there, it was almost like being in another century."

The others laughed.

"I wish Mrs. Holmes had been able to remember who brought her the letter," Violet remarked as the Aldens were mounting their bicycles.

"That would have made our job a little easier," Henry remarked as he began to pedal away.

Jessie was about to follow when she noticed a large blue car parked under some trees near the antique store's driveway. The car flashed its lights and began to move toward the Aldens.

"Who is that?" Jessie asked out loud.

The car pulled alongside Jessie, Violet, and Benny. "How about a ride home?" a deep voice asked.

"Mr. Ambrose!" Jessie was so startled she almost shouted.

"What are you doing here?" Benny wanted to know. He was right behind Jessie.

"I was out exploring the area," Mr. Ambrose answered smoothly.

"We don't want a ride home," Benny said firmly.

"It's true," Jessie agreed. "What would we do with our bicycles?"

"I would probably have room for them in my trunk," Mr. Ambrose answered.

"We still don't need a ride." Benny remained firm.

"Were you driving out here to visit the antique store?" Jessie asked. She stood with one foot on the ground, the other on a bicycle pedal.

"Uh, no," Mr. Ambrose answered.

"Have you ever been in this store before?" Jessie persisted.

"I was here once or twice when I first began my research," the author answered. Then he cleared his throat. "Well, if you don't need a ride, I really must be on my way," he added. Before the Aldens could say anything more, the author pulled the car away and sped down the road.

"You know I saw a big blue car like that following us to the antique store," Benny informed his family when they were back on Seymour's farm. The four were walking their bicycles to the shed to put them away.

"I noticed that car, too," Henry remarked. "I'm sure it was Blake's car."

"But why would he want to follow us?" Violet asked as she walked her bicycle beside Henry's.

"Well, if he is involved in these burglaries, he probably wants to find out how much we know," Henry suggested.

"And he probably doesn't want us to get in his way," Jessie added.

That evening, after dinner, Violet and Benny decided to take a walk in the orchard with one of Seymour's flashlights. Benny wanted to hear the ghost for himself, and Violet thought it might be good to keep him company.

It was a windy night and as Violet waved the flashlight at the scarecrow, it looked like he was waving at them.

"Poor scarecrow," Violet said sadly. "He's probably going to need to be restuffed after this windy night."

"I bet we'll hear the ghost tonight," Benny said eagerly. He walked into the orchard, with Violet at his heels. At that moment, the two heard some whispering, and a low call that sounded like a long, drawn-out *boooooo.*

"What's that?" Benny asked.

Violet listened closely.

"Whooooooo . . . Whooooooo . . . Whoooooo."

"It could be an owl," Violet answered, but she did not sound very sure. Being out in the orchard after dark was spookier than she had thought.

"No, it's not," Benny said stubbornly.

"How far do you want to go?" Violet asked.

"Not too far," Benny said. His voice was a little quavery as he peered into the dark mass of fruit trees whose branches looked as if they could reach out and grab him. "Are there wolves out here?" Benny wanted to know.

"I don't think so. In fact, I'm sure there aren't."

Just at that moment, Benny and Violet heard a long, low hiss. Benny jumped two feet in the air. "Do you hear that?" he shouted, clutching Violet's arm. "I bet that's a snake."

Violet stopped walking and shone her flashlight on some low bushes behind the trees. Stray leaves were rustling in the wind, making a hissing sound — *pssst, pssst, pssst.* "That might be the whispering sound we're hearing," Violet said hopefully.

"Are you sure?" Benny asked.

"Yes." Violet's voice quavered. She wasn't really sure, but she wanted Benny to believe she was.

To get their minds off the hissing noise, Violet shone her light, which was getting dimmer, on the trees in front of her. Something she saw made her stop short and stare. "Benny, that marking. It wasn't here the last time we were in the orchard."

"What marking?" Benny rushed over to the tree where the flashlight shone on its bark. In the dim light, he could see a drawing of a helmet, next to the drawing of the sword the Aldens had seen earlier.

"You're right," Benny said. "Do you think the ghost drew this?"

"No, I don't," Violet said. "But I hope it doesn't mean that a helmet is missing from Seymour's collection."

"Oh, I hadn't thought of that," Benny exclaimed. "We'd better check the secret passageway right away." At that moment, the flashlight went out. Violet and Benny could not believe how dark it seemed, even in the moonlight.

CHAPTER 9

By the Light of the Moon

"I'm scared," Benny admitted.

Violet gulped. "Take my hand. We're not far from the farm."

Guided by the moonlight, Violet and Benny made their way home, stumbling over rocks and large branches in their path.

"Things sure look different in the dark," Benny muttered as two bats fluttered over them.

"Ugh." Violet shuddered. She let go of Benny's hand and almost dropped her flashlight so she could cover her hair. "I can't stand bats."

Benny and Violet were very happy to see the farmhouse in the distance, lit with a warm light from the lamps in the living room.

Twenty minutes later, all the Aldens and Seymour were in the secret passageway. Carefully they shone their flashlights on all the suits of armor.

"Oh, no!" Violet groaned. Just as she had feared, one of the helmets was missing.

"That's the most valuable helmet in the collection." Seymour sounded angry. "That thief sure knows what he's doing."

That night, before they went to bed, Henry, Jessie, Violet, and Benny met in Jessie and Violet's bedroom. Jessie sat on the large bed, her notebook in hand. "We have to do something before anything else disappears," she said firmly. "At least we have some leads."

Henry nodded. "We suspect Blake Ambrose is involved."

"And someone from the farm must be helping him," Jessie added. "Remember, Seymour told us that only the farm workers know how to get inside the secret passageway. Someone from the farm must be involved, too."

"Now we just have to find out who," said Benny. He sat with his legs crossed on Jessie's bed.

"Blake knows Veronica," Violet said. "I wonder if he knows anyone else who could be helping him."

"I think Veronica and Blake are our two most likely suspects," Jessie said. "But we shouldn't forget about Martin, Mike, and Jeff. I think anyone who works in the orchard is a suspect."

"Oh, not Martin," Benny protested. "He's always been so nice to us."

"He has," Henry agreed. "But Martin does spend a lot of time with Veronica. And if she's involved, chances are he may be, also."

"I guess so," Violet said reluctantly.

"What have Mike and Jeff done to make

us suspicious?" Jessie asked. She was busy writing in the notebook with a green fountain pen.

"Well, they aren't very likely suspects," Henry admitted. "After all, Seymour has known them a long time, and we haven't caught them behaving suspiciously."

"No, they seem to work very hard," Jessie remarked. "Still, if we really want to find out what's going on, we should probably observe them as well."

The others nodded.

"Veronica and Martin are usually together, so it shouldn't be too hard to keep track of them," Jessie added. "Why don't Violet and I watch Martin and Veronica, and you two can observe Mike and Jeff," she said to Henry.

"That's fine with me," said Henry. "I don't want to deal with Veronica. It shouldn't be too hard to keep an eye on Mike and Jeff. They're usually in the orchard pruning trees."

"Who's going to watch Blake Ambrose?" Benny wanted to know.

"If he is working with someone from the

farm, we might as well wait and have one of the workers lead us to him," Jessie said.

"The only problem with this plan is that it could take a long time for us to catch the thief in action," Henry said.

"That's true," Jessie agreed.

"You know, I have an idea," Violet said quietly. The others turned to look at her. "The thieves must be making those markings on the tree late at night. I doubt anyone would try to mark it up during the daytime."

"True," Henry agreed.

"So," Violet continued, "why don't we camp out in the orchard late at night near that tree and see what happens."

Benny made a face.

"We'll take lots of flashlights this time," Violet said, looking at Benny. "And extra batteries."

"And extra sweaters and maybe blankets," added Jessie.

"It'll be too cold to camp out for the night," Henry said. "It's too bad we don't have a tent or something."

"A tent would be too noticeable," Jessie remarked.

"We should probably plan to do this tomorrow night," Henry said.

The others agreed.

The following day, Jessie and Violet tried to keep track of Veronica and Martin. Henry and Benny found many excuses to go into the orchard to help Mike and Jeff. No one noticed anything suspicious.

That night after dinner, the Aldens waited until everyone had gone to bed before creeping out to the orchard. After much discussion, they had decided not to tell Grandfather or Seymour of their plan. They knew Grandfather would worry, even though he trusted them to take care of themselves. And they were afraid Seymour would forbid them from going.

Tonight the moon was very full and low in the sky. "That's a Hunter's Moon," Henry said. "It usually comes out in the middle of November."

"It seems brighter out here than it was last night," Benny remarked.

"There aren't as many clouds," Violet observed. "But it's a lot colder."

"I'll say," Benny agreed as he stamped his feet to keep warm. He could see his breath in the cold night air. Violet pulled up the hood of her purple parka. Jessie rubbed her hands together.

"We won't get as cold if we keep moving," Henry suggested as he led the way into the orchard. As the Aldens walked past the scarecrow, they noticed he had fallen over and now lay in a crumpled heap on the ground. Benny noticed his clothes were missing.

"The farm probably doesn't even need a scarecrow this time of year," Jessie said. "Not much is growing."

"Once we're in the orchard, we should probably turn off our flashlights," Henry suggested. "We don't want to attract too much attention."

"But with all these trees around, it's hard to see," Benny pointed out.

"We'll guide you, if you need the help," Henry assured him as Benny obediently turned off his light.

"Don't those tree branches look like claws in the moonlight?" Benny pointed out.

"Oooh, they do," Jessie agreed, shuddering a little. "And what's that noise?"

"What noise?" Benny wanted to know.

"Sssh."

The four Aldens heard the sounds of twigs snapping, then a long, drawn-out, "Whooooooo."

"That's that owl we heard last night," Violet said.

"Whooooo. Whoooooo. Whoooooo."

"That doesn't sound like an owl," Jessie whispered to Violet.

At that moment, a scarecrow came out of the trees and appeared before the Aldens, waving his arms in the moonlight.

"Aaaagh!" Benny shrieked.

CHAPTER 10

Joshua's Ghost

"It's the ghost. It's Joshua!" Benny couldn't stop shrieking.

Just as suddenly as he appeared, the ghost vanished — with Henry chasing after him.

"Benny, Benny, calm down," Jessie said soothingly. She hugged Benny to her, while Violet buried her face in Jessie's arm.

"That was so scary," Violet groaned.

"I know it was," Jessie agreed. "I just hope Henry's okay."

"Do you think the ghost will try to hurt him?" Benny asked, looking very serious.

Jessie shook her head. "Benny, I don't think that was really a ghost."

A few minutes later, Henry appeared, looking discouraged. "He was too fast for me. He got away."

"You mean he vanished into the air," Benny said. He knew that was what ghosts did.

"No, he just ran too fast," Henry said as he turned on his flashlight. "But if we follow his path, maybe we can find some clues."

"Clues?" Benny asked.

"Yeah, like footprints or something," Henry said. He walked to the spot where the ghost had been and carefully studied the ground under his flashlight.

"But ghosts don't leave footprints," Benny protested.

"This one did," Henry called. "Look here."

In the ground in front of Henry were a set of extremely large footprints, much larger than Henry's.

"The man sure has big feet," Jessie remarked.

"And I think he wears hiking boots," Violet said as she beamed her flashlight on one of the footprints.

"Who do we know around here with feet that big, and hiking boots?" Henry asked.

"Not Mike!" Violet sounded shocked.

Henry nodded.

The following day, Henry, Jessie, Violet, and Benny were up early. They had not wanted to wake the others when they came in the night before. The first thing they did was talk to Seymour. They found him in the barn feeding the animals before breakfast.

"You did what? You went out after dark — alone — to try to catch a burglar?" Seymour did not sound happy. "You're lucky you didn't get hurt."

When Seymour had heard the whole story, he shook his head sadly. "I can't believe it's really Mike. I don't understand why he was trying to scare you like that, unless, as you say, he was trying to get you off his trail."

"I suppose it's possible it could be someone else with big feet and hiking boots," Jessie suggested.

"Let's hope so," Seymour said. "But the first thing we need to do is talk to Mike."

On their way out of the barn, Henry spotted something on the ground, under a bush. When he walked over, he saw it was a pile of clothing — the scarecrow's clothing.

"Come here," he called to the others. Henry picked up the large flannel shirt, the denim pants, and the black felt hat. "These are the clothes the scarecrow had on last night," Henry said, handing them to Seymour.

"I might as well take these back to the house," Seymour said. He sniffed the collar of the shirt. "That musky smell — do you recognize it?" he asked the Aldens.

"Sort of," said Jessie, wrinkling her nose. "But I can't place it."

"It's an aftershave Mike sometimes wears," Seymour said sadly.

Two hours later, the Aldens and Seymour found Mike in the orchard raking.

"I need to talk to you," Seymour told Mike. "Let's go up to the house." When Mike saw all the Aldens around Seymour, he turned pale and leaned his rake against the side of the tree.

"I think I know what all this is about," he said.

"There's no excuse for what I did," Mike said, looking at his hands. He sat at the kitchen table with Seymour, Henry, Jessie, Violet, and Benny.

"So you stole my things," Seymour said. He sounded more hurt than angry. "Mike, you've worked for me all these years. What happened? Did you need money?"

"I did. Rob is very sick. Rob's my son," he added for the Aldens' benefit. "He needs money for a kidney transplant. I guess I was desperate. When that guy approached me, wanting me to help him out, I didn't think. He offered me so much money I couldn't refuse."

"What guy?" Benny asked.

"That guy who's hanging around town pretending to be an author. He told me he met you in the library."

"Blake Ambrose," Benny said.

"Right."

"He's not really an author?" Henry sounded surprised.

Mike shrugged. "I think he's written a couple of horror stories that have sold well. But he makes most of his money stealing antiques and then selling them off to dealers in New York and Boston."

"So you helped him steal the things from here?" Henry asked.

Mike sighed. "Yes. I didn't steal from any other places. Blake would leave me messages carved on one of the trees. I would just take what he wanted me to. He'd given me a list of all the things he wanted from the farm when we agreed to work together."

"If he did that, why did he need to leave you the messages on the tree?" Benny asked.

"I couldn't take everything at the same time," Mike explained. "Blake wanted me to steal the items one at a time, when he was ready for them. He had an odd way of doing things. He hardly ever wanted us to be seen together."

"And you worked alone. I mean, no one else helped you?" Henry wanted to make sure.

"No, no one else was involved," Mike said. "And Blake told me that if the pieces I took didn't sell, I could get them back. I was keeping track of where the pieces went so I could return them to you, someday, if I ever got the money to buy them back," he said to Seymour.

Seymour nodded sadly. "Mike, you should have told me about Rob. I didn't know. I might have been able to help you some other way."

"I know, Seymour." Mike had tears in his eyes, which he tried to brush away. "As I said, I just wasn't thinking. I was so worried about my son."

"So you know where Seymour's things are?" Henry asked.

Mike nodded. "Most of the letters are with a dealer in Boston. So is the stamp collection. But the sword and helmet are still here in Chassell."

Violet looked puzzled. "How come a local antique store had one of the letters?" she asked.

"That was a slipup," Mike explained. "That letter got mixed in with some things I was taking to a yard sale — not any of the stolen goods, but some things from my house I was selling to help raise money. It was careless of me, I admit. Blake was really mad about that letter, especially after it ended up in the local paper. He almost didn't pay me because of it."

"It's funny Mrs. Holmes didn't remember buying that letter at a yard sale," Violet remarked.

"Mrs. Holmes is kind of absentminded," Mike said.

"She sure is," Seymour agreed, smiling for the first time all morning, but he was serious again when he turned to Mike. "You know, I'm going to have to call the police," he told his farmhand.

"I know," Mike said.

The police arrived twenty minutes later. "We're going to need you to write out a full confession," one of the police officers told Mike as he led him outside to the waiting car.

"I will," Mike said. "And I want to do all I can to get Seymour's things."

"The more you cooperate in this investigation, the lighter your sentence will be," the officer said.

That evening, the old black phone in the living room rang three times before Benny rushed to answer it.

"It's for you, Seymour," Benny called. "It's the police."

Benny waited by the phone hoping to hear some news, but the person on the other end of the line was doing most of the talking. "Yes. Yes," Seymour was saying.

"Good. Good. Really. Yes. Okay. Thank you."

Benny hopped on one foot, then the other. "What did they say?" he asked after Seymour hung up the phone.

"Well, thanks to Mike's help, the police caught up with Blake Ambrose just outside of Boston. He's wanted in five other states for burglary — all antiques. He's the one who did all the robberies in Chassell."

"Wow," said Benny.

"Are you getting your things back?" Jessie asked as she came into the kitchen, followed by Henry, Violet, Grandfather, Rose, Veronica, Martin, and Jeff.

"Yes. The police are working on that. Apparently my sword and helmet were in Blake's car, so I can have those right away. It may take longer to get the stamp collection and letters, but the police know where they are. And if the dealer has sold them, he's kept records. In time, I'm sure I'll get everything back."

"Thank goodness," Grandfather said.

"What's going to happen to Mike?" Benny wanted to know.

"Since it's his first offense and he cooperated with the police, he won't have to go to jail," Seymour said. "But he may have to do lots of community service."

Jeff shook his head. "I had no idea Mike was under so much financial pressure. He has been looking worried lately, but he keeps everything to himself, so it's hard to know what's really going on with him."

"If we'd known Mike was so desperate, we would have lent him money," Rose said. "We still can."

"I'm planning to," Seymour said.

"That's kind of you," Jeff said.

"What a story," Veronica commented, shaking her head. "Who would have thought all this was happening in this sleepy old orchard?"

"Veronica," Jessie said, "how did you know Blake Ambrose?"

"Oh, I didn't know him very well," Veronica said. "I used to see him in the library when I was there getting books for my history paper on the Civil War."

"Did he offer to help you with your research?" Henry asked.

"Yes," Veronica said, laughing. "I remember once he seemed kind of mad because I was taking out some books he said he needed. He sure knew a lot about the Civil War. He told me he was an expert on military history."

"That's probably how he knew so much about my sword and armor collection," Seymour remarked. "It is a relief to have this mystery solved."

"Well, one mystery is solved," Benny said. "But I still want to find out about Joshua's ghost."

Veronica rolled her eyes, but everyone else laughed.

The next three nights, Benny walked out to the orchard, sometimes alone, sometimes with Henry, Violet, or Jessie. Each night he heard a long, low boo. On the third night, Jessie convinced him it was really an owl when her flashlight spotlighted the bird in the tree.

"But what about that hissing sound Violet and I heard?" Benny asked.

"It could have been a snake," Jessie said. "But I bet it was the sound of leaves rustling."

"That's what Violet said." Benny sounded extremely discouraged. "You don't really think there's a ghost, do you?"

"No, I don't," Jessie answered.

Benny looked so crushed that Jessie put her arms around him.

The following morning, it rained. "Why don't we go to the shed to explore that buggy," Jessie suggested.

"Sure," Benny said. "I'll go."

"Be my guests," Seymour said, chuckling. "Let me know if you find anything interesting."

"There's tons of cool stuff in this buggy," Benny said as he looked through a box that held some old spinning tops, marbles, and a set of wooden blocks with letters and drawings carved into them.

"I bet those blocks are handmade," Jessie said. "Someone must have carved them for his children."

"Do you really think so?" Benny held up a block with the letter *D* carved on one side, and a dog on the other.

"It would have been a great way to teach a little kid the alphabet," Henry remarked. He sat inside the buggy poring over some old letters he had seen in one of the wooden chests.

Jessie and Violet were beside the buggy, carefully trying on old hats and petticoats they had found in the steamer trunk.

Benny blew dust off a marble and then dropped it. It fell inside the buggy. As he bent down to look for it, he noticed a long leather bag near his feet. Part of the bag was under a wooden box. Benny moved the box out of the way so he could pick up the bag.

Henry looked up from his reading. "That's a saddlebag," he told Benny. "People used to put them across a horse's shoulders in front of the saddle while riding, to carry stuff."

"Neat," said Benny. "Let's see what's in it." Benny pulled out a newspaper, very yellowed with age, that practically crumbled to pieces as he set it down. Then he took out an old seed catalog, and finally a letter in a long white envelope. The letter was addressed to Mr. Gideon Curtis!

"This letter has never been opened," Benny said. "Should we read it?"

"Maybe we should let Seymour open it," Henry suggested. "It's addressed to his ancestor."

"Look, it's got a Virginia postmark," Jessie said, looking over Benny's shoulder. The feathers in her hat tickled his nose.

"Aaa-choo!"

"A Virginia postmark," Henry said, reaching for the letter. "Maybe it's from Joshua!"

The Aldens lost no time finding Seymour. He was sitting at the kitchen table having a cup of coffee with Grandfather and Rose.

"I never knew there was a saddlebag in that buggy," Seymour said as he opened the letter, which was written in ink. "It *is* from Joshua!"

"What does it say?" Benny was so impatient, he was hopping up and down.

Seymour cleared his throat and began reading:

Virginia
18 November 1865

Dear Cousin,

It has now been eight years since I last saw you. I have not written because I was still very angry we could never come to an agreement about your father's sword & armor collection, & then the War began. I left your house in a huff, & it has taken me years to stop being so angry. I regret the time we've lost, when we once so enjoyed each other's company, but so be it. I am writing now to tell you I plan to leave the country. The War has left my house and land in ruins & there is nothing left for me here. I plan to go abroad & hope to settle in Australia.

Cousin, as I will probably never see you again, I write to wish you well. Love to Sybil, Theodore, and Alice.

Faithfully yours,
Joshua

"My goodness. And this letter has been in the barn all the time! Gideon never opened it. He must have picked up his mail on horseback one time, put it in his saddle-bag, and then forgot about it," Rose suggested.

"It's strange he would have forgotten a letter from Joshua," Seymour said. "Maybe he wasn't the one who picked up the mail."

"He never knew his cousin had forgiven him," Violet said.

"Australia. No wonder no one ever heard from him." Seymour couldn't believe it.

"I guess that means Joshua was never really a ghost," Benny said sadly.

"I'm afraid not, Benny." Seymour shook his head.

"Maybe the ghost isn't really Joshua?" Violet teased.

Benny perked up. "I never thought of that."

Everyone laughed.

GERTRUDE CHANDLER WARNER discovered when she was teaching that many readers who like an exciting story could find no books that were both easy and fun to read. She decided to try to meet this need, and her first book, *The Boxcar Children*, quickly proved she had succeeded.

Miss Warner drew on her own experiences to write the mystery. As a child she spent hours watching trains go by on the tracks opposite her family home. She often dreamed about what it would be like to set up housekeeping in a caboose or freight car — the situation the Alden children find themselves in.

When Miss Warner received requests for more adventures involving Henry, Jessie, Violet, and Benny Alden, she began additional stories. In each, she chose a special setting and introduced unusual or eccentric characters who liked the unpredictable.

While the mystery element is central to each of Miss Warner's books, she never thought of them as strictly juvenile mysteries. She liked to stress the Aldens' independence and resourcefulness and their solid New England devotion to using up and making do. The Aldens go about most of their adventures with as little adult supervision as possible — something else that delights young readers.

Miss Warner lived in Putnam, Connecticut, until her death in 1979. During her lifetime, she received hundreds of letters from girls and boys telling her how much they liked her books.